A CLOAK
FOR THE
MOON

retold by Eric A. Kimmel

illustrated by Katya Krenina

Holiday House / *New York*

Text copyright © 2001 by Eric A. Kimmel
Illustrations copyright © 2001 by Katya Krenina
All Rights Reserved
Printed in the United States of America
www.holidayhouse.com
First Edition
The text typeface is Kennerly.
The artwork was prepared in gouache.

Library of Congress Cataloging-in-Publication Data
Kimmel, Eric A.
A cloak for the moon / retold by Eric A. Kimmel; illustrated by Katya Krenina.—1st ed.
p. cm.
Summary: A retelling of one of Rabbi Nachman's tales
in which a tailor, dreaming that the moon is cold in the sky,
goes in search of a special fabric
with which to make it a cloak.
ISBN 0-8234-1493-0
[1. Tailors—Fiction. 2. Moon—Fiction.
3. Jews—Fiction. 4. Parables.]
I. Krenina, Katya, ill. II. Title.
PZ7.K5648Ci 2001
[Fic]—dc21 CIP
99-016697

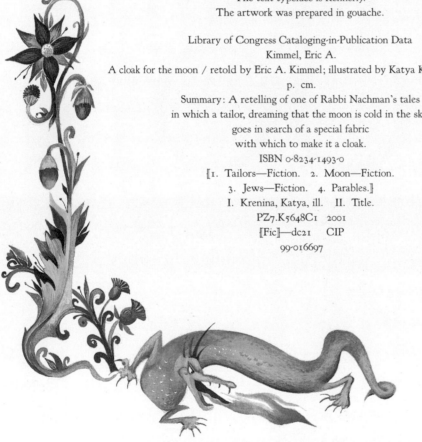

For my grandfather
Morris Isaac Kerker,
who prized fine stories
and fine tailoring.
E. A. K.

To the caring and loving
Breytburg family,
my wonderful friends.
K. K.

A TAILOR ONCE LIVED in the city of Tzafat. Haskel was his name.
He spent his days sewing fine clothes for the people of the town.
At night he climbed to the roof of his house, where he lay for hours,
watching the moon. He never tired of looking at her.

One night, as Haskel lay on the roof, he had a dream. He saw the moon shivering. "Ay, Haskel," she sighed. "I am so cold. How I wish I had a cloak to keep me warm!"

"I will make you a cloak, dear Moon!" Haskel cried. He suddenly found himself awake. "Dream or not, I will keep my promise," Haskel told himself. "I will sew the moon a cloak of shining silver thread. All the stars will envy her."

The next morning Haskel went to visit his
uncle, a master tailor. No secret in the tailor's art was hidden from him.

"How does one make a cloak for the moon?" Haskel asked.

"Why make one cloak? Why not two? Then the sun can have one,"
said his uncle.

"The sun doesn't need a cloak. He shines in the day, when the air
is warm. But the moon is so cold up in the night sky. I promised to
make her a cloak, but I don't know how to begin."

Haskel's uncle feared his nephew might be losing his wits. "There is no way to begin. A tailor must measure his customer before making the garment. How will you measure the moon? Even if you could, the moon never stays the same. She wanes and waxes. A cloak that fits her one day will be too big or small the day after. Stop chasing dreams, Haskel. You can't make a cloak for the moon. No one can."

Haskel left, deeply disappointed. As he turned down the street, he heard someone call his name. "Haskel! Haskel!"

It was Ephraim, one of his uncle's apprentices. "I overheard what you asked. I know something that might help. I once mended a coat for a silk merchant, who told me stories of his journeys. In a distant land, he said, there is a garment woven with beams of light. It has no weight at all and perfectly fits whoever wears it. If the person is large, it stretches. If the person is small, it shrinks."

"That is exactly what I need!" Haskel exclaimed. "Tell me, Ephraim, where can this fabric be found?"

"I cannot help you," Ephraim replied. "The man did not tell me that."

"I will find it some way," Haskel said.

Haskel closed his shop and set out on a journey. He walked to the port city of Aqaba. There he boarded a ship bound for China. The most wonderful fabrics in the world could be found there: radiant satins, silks like colored water, and a marvelous cloth that would not burn, even when placed in a roaring fire.

Haskel's ship arrived in the city of Zaitun. He asked everyone he met, but no one knew anything about a fabric woven from beams of light.

Then a Persian trader drew him aside, whispering,
"I've heard of this cloth you seek. It comes from a city
high in the mountains called The Roof of the World."

Haskel joined a caravan bound for the town of Kunming. He crossed stony deserts and wild, surging rivers. When the caravan reached its destination, he continued on alone.

Haskel struggled through steep mountain passes. After countless perils, he arrived at the city called The Roof of the World.

Crowds of people filled the streets, but no one smiled or laughed. The people looked as if they were living their last day.

"Why are you all so sad?" Haskel asked a glassblower.

"We grieve for our beloved princess," the glassblower told him.

"Did she die?"

"No, heaven forbid! Our princess has no wedding dress."

"Is she getting married?"

"Ah, that's the problem! You see, Stranger, our queen possesses a wonderful dress. It is woven from beams of light. There is nothing like it in the world. Every queen as far back as anyone can remember has given her daughter that dress to wear on her wedding day. The dress always shrinks or stretches to fit the bride. Alas! The dress has become unraveled. None of our tailors can mend it. And without the dress, our princess cannot be married. That is why everyone is so sad."

"Maybe I can help. Where can I find the queen's palace?" Haskel asked the glassblower.

"Follow this street. It will take you there."

Haskel followed the street to the palace gate. "Take me to the queen," he told the guards. "I may be able to help her."

The guards brought Haskel to the queen. "O Queen," he said, "I am a tailor from a distant land. If your dress can be mended at all, I believe I can do it."

"This dress is like no other," the queen cautioned. "It is woven from beams of light. The hem has become unraveled. Once the thread unravels, it disappears. No one can mend the dress because there is nothing to mend. More thread is needed, but the secret of spinning thread from light has been lost."

Haskel trembled with excitement. If he could discover that secret, he could make a cloak for the moon.

"May I examine the dress?" he asked the queen.

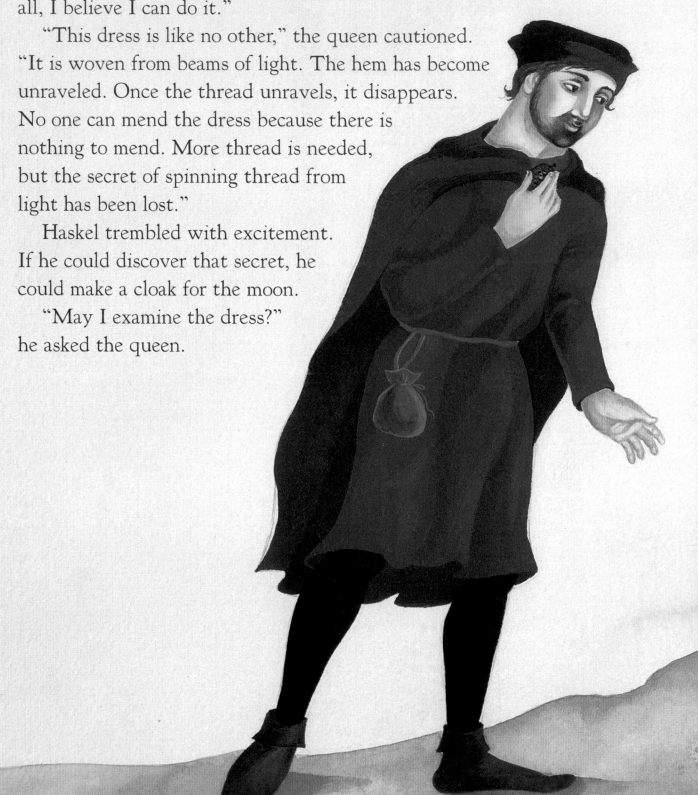

The queen took Haskel to a private room. A servant brought the dress to him in a sealed box. Haskel broke the seal. Never had he seen a garment like this! It was woven all in one piece and glowed as if spun from moonlight. Haskel put his arm through one sleeve. It fit perfectly!

"Everything I have heard about this dress is true," he said to himself. "Now, if only I can discover how it was made."

Haskel untied the bundle holding the tools of his trade: scissors, needles, tailor's chalk, measuring tape, and a small magnifying glass for counting thread. He examined the unraveled hem under the glass. As he pulled the loose thread, it turned to light and disappeared.

Haskel did not notice the hours passing. The moon arose, filling the room with silver light. Haskel sat by the window to see better. His magnifying glass focused the moonlight shining through the window into a tiny beam. As the beam touched the end of the thread, it began to spin. Before Haskel's astonished eyes, the beam spun itself into thread, the thread wove itself into cloth, and the hem of the garment began to lengthen. "So that is the secret!" he murmured to himself.

The dress was woven of moonlight, but the light had to be focused and guided for the magic to work.

When the wedding dress had reached its proper length, Haskel clipped off the end of the thread. He wrapped it in a handkerchief and put it in his pocket.

At dawn Haskel brought the wedding dress to the queen, who summoned her daughter. The dress fit perfectly. The princess wept with joy, for now that the miraculous dress was restored, her long-delayed wedding could take place.

The queen turned to Haskel. "I owe you a great debt. How may I repay you?"

Haskel replied, "O Queen, you do not owe me anything. I ask only that I be allowed to keep a small bit of thread that I clipped from the garment."

"It is yours," the queen said.

Haskel packed his tailor's bundle and began the long journey
home. Whenever the moon shined bright in the sky, he focused his
magnifying glass on the tiny bit of thread.

Night after night, the thread lengthened. It wove itself into cloth.
By the time Haskel reached Tzafat, he had many yards.

Once there he sewed a cloak for the moon, just as he had promised. It was a wonderful cloak that fit her perfectly as she waxed and waned. For the cloak was like the moon: beautiful and ever changing.

And how did Haskel deliver the cloak? He climbed a ladder of moonbeams that led to the sky.

There he can be seen to this day, sitting beside his beloved moon, wrapped in a cloak of silver light that is always wide enough for two.

AUTHOR'S
NOTE

This story is based on one of the tales of Rabbi Nachman
of Bratslav (1772–1811).
Rabbi Nachman was a gifted writer
as well as a great spiritual leader.
The mystical stories that he wrote for his followers are
among the finest works of Jewish literature.

ARTIST'S
NOTE

Eric A. Kimmel's beautiful retelling
of Rabbi Nachman's story appeals to me
on many levels. My goal was
to keep the mystical feeling
alive in my art.